D0538187

This book belongs to:

....

....

SWANSEA LIBRARIES

6000270627

CITY AND COUNTY OF
SWANSEA LIBRARIES

6000270627	
Askews & Holts	24-May-2016
	£4.99
LL	

Editor: Carly Madden
Designer: Rachel Lawston & Chloë Forbes
Editorial Director: Victoria Garrard
Art Director: Laura Roberts-Jensen

Copyright © QED Publishing 2015

First published in the UK in 2015 by QED Publishing
Part of The Quarto Group
The Old Brewery, 6 Blundell Street, London, N7 9BH

www.qed-publishing.co.uk

All rights reserved. No part of this publication may be reproduced, stored in a retrieval system,
or transmitted in any form or by any means, electronic, mechanical, photocopying, recording, or
otherwise, without the prior permission of the publisher, nor be otherwise circulated in any form
of binding or cover other than that in which it is published and without a similar condition
being imposed on the subsequent purchaser.

A catalogue record for this book is available from the British Library.

ISBN 978 1 78493 246 6

Printed in China

Monty the Hero

Steve Smallman

Monty Mole was reading his
favourite bedtime story.

It was the one about a hero,
a monster and a magic wand that
made wishes come true.

"I'm going to be a hero!"
said Monty.

"You can be a hero tomorrow," said his
mum, "but now it's time to sleep."

But Monty was
too excited
to sleep.

He tossed and turned until he
was sure it must be tomorrow.

So he got out of bed
and tunnelled up
and up until...

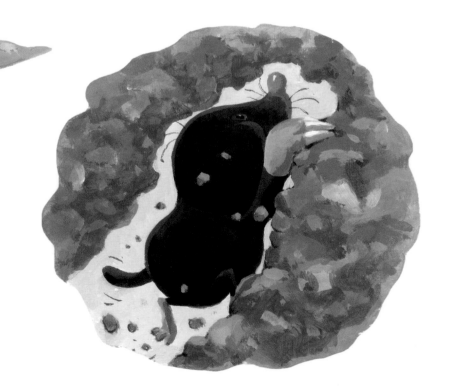

...he was in the **magical** land from his book!

"Hello!" said a friendly
voice. "I'm Herbert Hedgehog.
What are you doing up here?"

"I'm Monty Mole and I'm going to be a hero. You can be one too!"

"Great!" said Herbert.

Monty found a conker shell and put it on his head.

"In case we meet any monsters," he said.

Just then...

"IT'S A MONSTER!" squealed Monty.

Herbert rolled into
a spiky ball.

Monty stood very still
and held his breath.

"Hmmm, what have we here?" growled a grumpy badger.

"I'm a m... m... mushroom," squeaked Monty.

Suddenly Herbert stuck out his bottom
and prickled the badger's nose!

"OUCH!" it yelped and lumbered away.

"Wow!" said Monty.
"You really are a hero!"

"And you really are a **mushroom!**" laughed Herbert.

"NO, I'M NOT!" Monty shouted. "I'M A HERO!"

"MUSHROOM,
MUSHROOM,"
teased Herbert,
who scampered
off, laughing...

...and
fell
down
a
hole!

"HELP!" he cried.

Monty quickly dug down
until he found his friend.

"Thanks, Monty!" gasped Herbert.
"You're my hero!"

"Now we need to find the magic wand that makes wishes come true!" said Monty.

"Oh, look!" cried Herbert...

"How does it work?" whispered Herbert.

"I think you have to shake it," said Monty.

So they did...

...and all the magic suddenly flew up and drifted off on the breeze.

"Oh no!" cried Monty. "Catch it!"

The magic twirled and danced in
the air until... it disappeared.

"The magic's gone," sobbed Monty.
"I never even made a wish! I wish
my mum was here," he sniffled.

And suddenly...

...she was!

"Wow!" said Herbert. "It worked! Goodbye, Mushroom!" he chuckled.

"Mushroom?" asked Monty's mum.

"It's a long story," explained Monty.

Monty told his mum a story about
heroes, a monster, a magic wand
and a wish that came true...

...but he left out the part about the **mushroom!**

Next Steps

Show the children the cover again. When they first saw it, what sort of adventure did they think Monty might have?

Monty's mum was reading his favourite bedtime story. Did the story make Monty want to have an adventure of his own? Do the children sometimes wish that they could do things that people in stories do? What sort of things?

Was the 'monster' that came along really a monster? What did Herbert do that made Monty call him 'a real hero'?

How did Monty feel when Herbert teased him and shouted "Mushroom, mushroom." Ask the children how they would feel if their friends were teasing them.

What did Monty do that made Herbert call him a hero? Can you be a hero even if you are not big and strong?

Monty and Herbert found a magic wand. Was it really magic? Did it really make Monty's mum appear? Ask the children to draw a picture of what they would do if they had a magic wand.